This is for my family, for Granny Savory, for Frank Johnson, and
for all the ancestors making beautiful quilts out of rags and pieces.

RG

Dedicated to A, O, and D and to all those before me who,
despite it all, never lost hope.

MM

First edition 2022

Library of Congress Catalog Card Number 2021953318
ISBN 978-1-5362-2252-4

22 23 24 25 26 27 APS 10 9 8 7 6 5 4 3 2 1

Printed in Humen, Dongguan, China

This book was typeset in Filosophia.
The illustrations were created digitally.

Candlewick Press
99 Dover Street
Somerville, Massachusetts 02144

www.candlewick.com

Build a House

Rhiannon Giddens

illustrated by
Monica Mikai

CANDLEWICK PRESS

You brought me here
To build your house
To build your house
To build your house.

You brought me here
To build your house
And grow your garden
Fine.

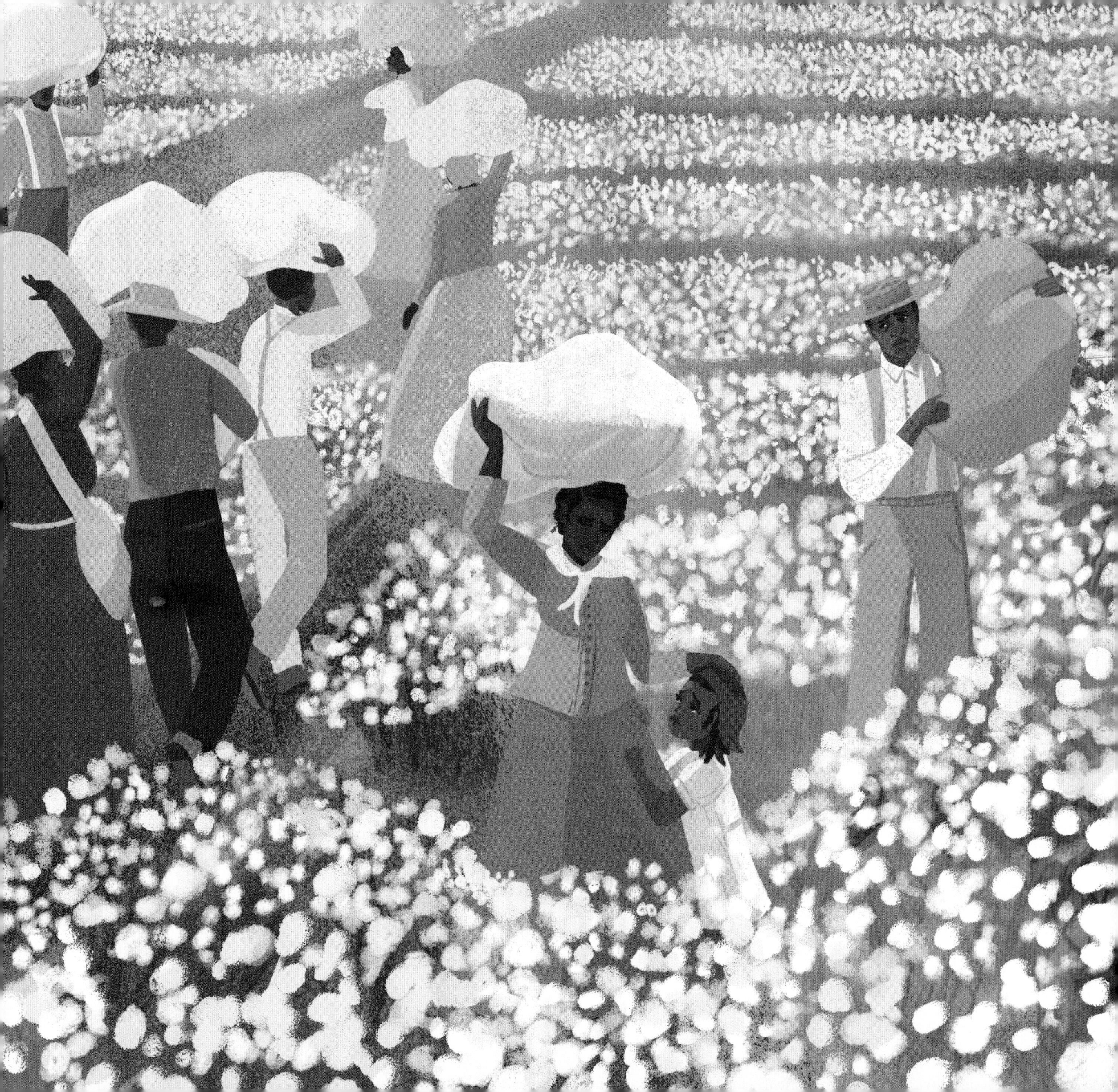

I laid the brick
To build your house
        To build your house
                To build your house.

I laid the brick
To build your house

And raised the plants so high.

And then you had the house and land

The house and land
The house and land.

And then you had
The house and land
And then you told me . . .

So I found a place
To build my house
To build my house
To build my house.

But you said I couldn't
Build a house

And so you burnt it . . .

DOWN.

I learned your words
And wrote my song
     Wrote my song
          Wrote my song.

But then you came
And took my song
And claimed it for your
Own.

So then I traveled
Far and wide

Far and wide

Far and wide.

So then I traveled

Far and wide

Until I found a
Home.

I took my bucket
Lowered it down
    Lowered it down
        Lowered it down.

I took my bucket
Lowered it down—

The well will never run
Dry.

I learned your words
And wrote my song
Wrote my song
Wrote my song.

I learned your words and wrote my song
I put my story down.

You brought me here
To build a house
    Build a house
        Build a house.

You brought me here
To build a house

And I will not be moved.

— AFTERWORD —

For a very long time, all over the world, people have been enslaved and forced to work for the people who enslaved them—it is one of the worst things about being human. But this story is not just about that—this story also shows one of the best things about being human: how we keep finding ways to make our family and our home, no matter where we are . . . no matter what. I am proud to be a banjo-playing descendant of the Afro-Carolinians who, against all the odds, made a culture and built a home and survived, so I could thrive.

Rhiannon Giddens

To hear a special performance of "Build a House" by Rhiannon Giddens and cellist Yo-Yo Ma, which was recorded for this book, please activate this QR code. View the code through the camera app on your phone. You can focus on the QR code by gently tapping on your screen. Follow the pop-up instructions to open the link.

This song was originally released in June 2020 to honor the 155th anniversary of Juneteenth (short for "June Nineteenth"), a holiday that commemorates the abolishment of slavery in the United States. On June 19, 1865, federal soldiers arrived in Galveston, Texas, to take control of the state, which had largely avoided the fighting during the Civil War. More than two years after the Emancipation Proclamation and more than two months after the Confederate surrender at Appomattox, the last still-enslaved peoples in the US finally learned that the war had ended and that they were free. This day, Juneteenth, has been celebrated in Black communities since the 1800s and finally became a national holiday in 2021.